The Gingerbread Man

Robert James and Bruno Robert

W

FRANKLIN WATTS

LONDON•SYDNEY

Once upon a time, there was a little old lady who loved to bake.
One hot day, she decided to bake a gingerbread man.

The little old lady
used currants
to make the
gingerbread man
some eyes. She
used a shiny,
red cherry to
make his
nose.

She was very hungry,
so she carefully popped
the gingerbread man
into the oven to bake.

The smell coming from the oven was delicious. "Mmmm," thought the little old lady, "I can't wait any more. I'm sure he's ready now."

She opened

the oven door

to check …

… and the gingerbread man jumped straight out of the oven! "Don't eat me!" cried the gingerbread man.

The little old lady and her husband couldn't believe their eyes.

The gingerbread man jumped up onto the shelf and out onto the windowsill.

"Stop!" shouted the little old lady. "I'm very hungry and I want to eat you up!"

"Run, run as fast as you can! You can't catch me, I'm the gingerbread man!" cried the gingerbread man. He ran straight up the garden path and out of the gate.

13

The little old lady and her husband chased the gingerbread man to a grassy meadow, but they couldn't catch him.

In the meadow, there
was a hungry cow.
"Stop!" mooed the cow.
"I'm very hungry and I
want to eat you up!"

But the gingerbread man jumped
straight over the cow's nose.
"Run, run as fast as you can!
You can't catch me, I'm the
gingerbread man!" he cried.

17

The cow, the little old lady and her husband chased the gingerbread man to a stable yard, but they couldn't catch him.

In the yard, there was a hungry horse. "Stop!" neighed the horse. "I'm very hungry and I want to eat you up!"

But the gingerbread man jumped up onto a fence post. "Run, run as fast as you can! You can't catch me, I'm the gingerbread man!" he cried.

21

The horse, the cow, the little old lady and her husband chased the gingerbread man to a river, but they couldn't catch him.

"Oh no!" cried the gingerbread man.
"I can't swim so I can't cross the river.
They will catch me now."

Now a sly, old fox had been watching
this chase. He wanted to eat the
gingerbread man too. He had a plan.

"Do you want to cross the river?"
he asked the gingerbread man.
"Yes, and quickly!" the gingerbread
man replied.

"Well, jump up onto my head and I will swim across the river with you," said the sly, old fox.

"You promise not to eat me up?"
said the gingerbread man.
"Yes, yes," replied the sly, old fox,
not making any promise at all.

The gingerbread man jumped up
onto the sly, old fox's head.

The fox threw back his head, tossing the gingerbread man high into the air. Then he opened his mouth and ... Snap!

That was the end of the gingerbread man.

About the story

The Gingerbread Man story is one of many traditional tales about food that runs away. The character of a gingerbread man first appeared in an American magazine called *St Nicholas* in 1875.

An earlier version of the tale was around in the 1840s involving a pancake. Joseph Jacobs published a version of the tale with a rolling cake called "Johnny-Cake" in his *English Fairy Tales* in 1890.

Be in the story!

Imagine you are the gingerbread
man just when he
jumps onto the
fox's head.

What will you
say to the fox
to make sure he
doesn't gobble you up?
Can you think of a clever way to
trick the fox just like he tricks the
gingerbread man?

First published in 2014 by
Franklin Watts
338 Euston Road
London
NW1 3BH

Franklin Watts Australia
Level 17/207 Kent Street
Sydney
NSW 2000

A CIP catalogue record for this book is available
from the British Library.

The artwork for this story first appeared in
Leapfrog: The Gingerbread Man

ISBN 978 1 4451 2819 1 (hbk)
ISBN 978 1 4451 2820 7 (pbk)
ISBN 978 1 4451 2822 1 (library ebook)
ISBN 978 1 4451 2821 4 (ebook)

Series Editor: Jackie Hamley
Series Advisor: Catherine Glavina
Series Designer: Cathryn Gilbert

Printed in China

Franklin Watts is a divison of
Hachette Children's Books,
an Hachette UK company.
www.hachette.co.uk